Women Who Rock

MISTY Copeland

GAIL TERP

BLACK RABBIT BOOKS

Bolt is published by Black Rabbit Books
P.O. Box 227, Mankato, Minnesota, 56002.
www.blackrabbitbooks.com

Design and Production by Michael Sellner
Photo Research by Rhonda Milbrett

Library of Congress Control Number: 2015954915

HC ISBN: 978-1-68072-065-5 PB ISBN: 978-1-68072-315-1

Printed in the United States of America

Image Credits

AP Images: Evan Agostini/Invision, 32; Kevin Karzin, 11; Corbis: Joe Stevens/Retna Ltd, Back Cover, 1, 6, 26; Raymond Hagans/Retna Ltd, 8 (right); danceinsoul.com: 12 (top); Getty: Carolyn Cole, Cover, 16–17, 18; Gabriel Olsen, 8–9 (left); Hiroyuki Ito, 20–21; Mireya Acierto, 22; Mireya Acierto, 25 (top); iStock: Antonio Gravante, 14–15 (dancers); Newscom: MCMULLAN CO/SIPA, 9 (right); Shutterstock: doodko, 31; Pressmaster, 3, 28–29; Vereshchagin Dmitry, 14–15 (background); ykononova, 13, 26–27; thandiekay.com: 12 (bottom); Wikimedia: Gilda N. Squire-Squire Media & Management, Inc., 24, 25 (bottom); Naim Chidiac Abu Dhabi Festival, 4–5
Every effort has been made to contact copyright holders for material reproduced in this book. Any omissions will be rectified in subsequent printings if notice is given to the publisher.

Contents

CHAPTER 1

Principal Dancer

The stage lights shine down. The music begins. Misty Copeland leaps onto the stage. High on her toes, she steps and hops. She kicks high, and her toes seem to touch the sky. Her spins last forever. When Copeland takes her bow, the audience roars. Bravo!

Superstar

Copeland is a ballerina. She dances with the American Ballet Theatre (ABT). In 2015, she was named an ABT **principal** dancer. Some people didn't want her to have that honor. They said ballet was only for white dancers. They said ballerinas should be tall and thin. Copeland is short and African American. And she proved those people wrong. She is a powerful, beautiful dancer.

Fun Facts

WROTE 2 BOOKS

HAS 5 SIBLINGS

5 feet
2 inches
(1.6 m) tall

LOVES TO EAT SUSHI

weighs
112 pounds
(51 kg)

ENJOYS
COOKING

CHAPTER 2

Early Years

Copeland was born September 10, 1982. She lived with her mother and her five siblings. They were quite poor. Copeland began to dance ballet at age 13. She loved it. But most ballet dancers start before they are 8. Copeland had lots of catching up to do. She worked hard. It was soon clear she was a talented dancer.

Always Dancing

Copeland's dancing got better and better. And her goals grew. She wanted to dance with the ABT. For two years, she went to the ABT summer program. The teachers were **impressed** with her.

After only two years of dancing, Copeland won the Spotlight Award. This award is given to artists who have great talent.

BALLET POSITIONS

Copeland had to learn the basic positions of ballet.

3rd
Position
4th
Position
5th
Position

CHAPTER 3

Making It Big

In 2000, ABT showed how much they liked Copeland's dancing. The leaders asked her to join the group. Copeland was now an ABT ballerina!

The next year, Copeland moved up to their **corps de ballet**. She was proving she was a great dancer. She set a new goal. She wanted to be the group's first African American principal dancer.

COPELAND BY THE NUMBERS

4
MILLION

YOUTUBE VIEWS IN ONE WEEK OF A COMMERCIAL FEATURING HER

1

METAL PLATE WAS PUT IN HER LEG

A Problem

Things were going well for Copeland. But there was one problem. She ate too much junk food. Her body was heavier than she wanted. It was hard to dance her best.

Copeland had to make a change. She learned how her body works. And she learned how to eat right. Today, her body is in top shape.

26 SECONDS — TIME IT TAKES HER TO PUT ON HER POINTE SHOES

Reaching Another Goal

In 2007, Copeland became an ABT **soloist**. She danced bigger roles. In 2012, she starred in *The Firebird*. Copeland danced her heart out. But she was in pain. After a week, she had to stop dancing. She had six cracks in her left leg bone. Copeland couldn't dance for seven months.

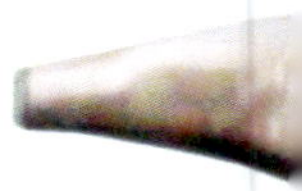

The injury didn't stop her, though. When she came back, she danced better than ever. ABT leaders took note. In June 2015, they made Copeland a principal dancer!

P.S./I. 84
GJS

CHAPTER 4

Copeland Today

When Copeland was young, her family didn't have much. Many people helped her. Now, Copeland wants to be the one who helps. She and ABT started Project Plié. The program gives ballet lessons to kids who can't afford them.

Life in Motion

Copeland knows her story can **inspire** others. To share her story, she wrote *Life in Motion*. In her book, she tells of her drive to be a ballerina. She also wrote a children's book called *Firebird*.

Copeland **mentors** several dancers. She helps them deal with the tough training. And she gives them advice.

FIREBIRD

Inspiring Today

MENTORING DANCERS

LIFE IN MOTION

AWARDS

2008
Leonore Annenberg Fellowship in the Arts

2013
National Youth of the Year Ambassador for the Boys and Girls Club

2014
Member of the President's Council on Fitness, Sports, and Nutrition

2015
Time Magazine's 100 Most Influential People

In the Spotlight

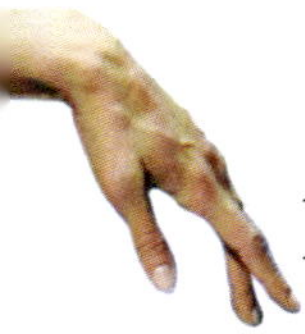

Copeland helps ballet reach more people. She has proven that skin color should not stop a dancer. No one can doubt she has star power. And she's likely to stay in the spotlight for years to come.

TIMELINE

1982
born in Missouri

1997-1998
dances in ABT summer programs

1999

2000
joins ABT

2001
moves up to corps de ballet

2002

2003

2004

2005

2007
becomes a soloist

2014
joins the President's Council on Fitness, Sports, and Nutrition

releases two books

2015
becomes an ABT principal dancer

GLOSSARY

corps de ballet (COR DAY bal-EY)—a permanent group of dancers in a ballet theater who are not soloists

impress (im-PRES)—to gain interest or admiration

inspire (in-SPIHR)—to make someone want to do something

mentor (MEN-tor)—to act as a teacher or guide

pointe (POYNT)—a ballet position where a dancer stands on the ends of the toes

principal (PRIN-suh-puhl)—at the highest rank

sibling (SI-bling)—a brother or sister

soloist (SO-lo-ist)—someone who performs by herself or himself

BOOKS

Copeland, Misty. *Firebird: Ballerina Misty Copeland Shows a Young Girl How to Dance Like the Firebird.* New York: G. P. Putnam's Sons, 2014.

Corman, Richard. *Misty Copeland: Power and Grace.* New York: Michael Friedman Group, 2015.

Hackett, Jane. *How to … Ballet: A Step-By-Step Guide to the Secrets of Ballet.* New York: DK, 2011.

WEBSITES

ABT: Dancers
www.abt.org/dancers/default.asp

Ballet Terms
wish-upon-a-ballet.com/ballet-terms/

Radacadabra
www.radacadabra.org/

INDEX